LUCKEY K.D.

Grimmwood Manor

A legacy of Fear

"In the shadows of forgotten places, where history's whispers turn to screams, the past is never truly buried. At Grimmwood Manor, fear is not a memory—it is a legacy."

Luckey K.D.

Contents

1

THE HIRING

My name is Dr. Emily Rawlins. I'm a psychiatrist. For the last ten years, I worked at a big hospital in the city, which was loud, crowded, and stressful.

Every day was the same. I woke up before sunrise, put on my suit, and hurried out the door. The commute was horrible - bumper-to-bumper traffic, blaring horns, stressed-out people everywhere.

When I finally made it to the hospital, it was chaos. My daily schedule was full of back-to-back patient appointments with no breaks. The patients all had major mental health issues - depression, anxiety, trauma, you name it. Hearing their sad stories and trying to help them heal was mentally draining work.

In addition to my patient load, there were piles of paperwork and endless meetings about hospital policies and insurance red tape. My boss was a total jerk, too, always telling me to be "more productive." The other doctors and I were just dollar signs to the hospital executives.

The days blurred together. I never had time for real life outside of work. My apartment was just a sad little place I returned to each night, exhausted, to briefly recharge before repeating the grind again. I was a shell of my former self, beaten down by the daily rat race.

Then one fateful night, it finally hit me how miserable I was. Sitting alone on my couch, eating greasy takeout at 10 pm after a 14-hour shift, I just cried. What was the point of killing myself at this soul-sucking job? I didn't even recognize myself anymore - I was so cynical, unhappy, and lost.

That was my breaking point. I knew something had to give before I had a complete mental breakdown myself. I needed to escape the chaos and find peace and balance again. My life needed a total 180 - a remote job away from the noise and stress of urban life. It was time to leave the city behind.

After my breakdown, I started looking online for new job opportunities. I spent hours scrolling through bland corporate listings that made me want to pull my hair out. Nothing felt right. Then, one peculiar job posting jumped out at me.

It was for a residential psychiatric clinic called Grimmwood Manor, located miles away in the remote hills. The ad described it as a peaceful healing retreat surrounded by nature and forests. The holistic approach combined therapy with outdoorsy activities like hiking, gardening, and animal care to promote wellness. No more dingy city hospital!

As I read more, some oddities caught my attention. The clinic was looking to hire multiple positions at once—psychiatrists, therapists, nurses, and support staff. It mentioned that the previous employees had "moved on" to other opportunities. How many people just up and left this place?

Other little things seemed strange, too. The website looked outdated, and the photos were obviously years ago. And why was this place so far out in the middle of nowhere hills? Was it somehow...cut off from society?

A nagging voice in my head wondered if I was diving head-first into another bad situation blind. After the soul-sucking misery of my city job, did I really want to risk getting stuck in a creepy, isolated clinic with a shady work history? Maybe I was just desperate for any change.

But the idea of living surrounded by pure nature, clean air, and peace and quiet sang to my inner spirit. No more concrete jungle, just me helping people find healing in a calming wooded environment. It seemed too idyllic to pass up after my breaking point.

Despite some reservations, I decided to take a risk and apply for the psychiatrist role at Grimmwood Manor. If it seemed sketchy, I could always leave. But this could be the fresh start and self-renewal I desperately craved. I fired off my resume and crossed my fingers.

A few days later, I got an email inviting me for an interview at Grimmwood Manor. I quickly mapped the directions - it was way further out in the mountains than I expected. Just getting there would be an adventure.

The journey took me up windy roads, deeper and deeper into the secluded hills. The scenery shifted from suburbs to thick forests with towering pines all around. I felt like I was entering another world entirely.

Finally, after what felt like ages, I crested a hill and saw it—Grimmwood Manor. It was an immense, rambling old stone building with ivy creeping up its walls. The overgrown grounds surrounded by shadowy woods gave it an aura of ancient decay.

As I drove up the cracked asphalt path, an uneasy feeling churned in my gut. This place seemed…off, cut off from the outside world entirely. What was I getting myself into?

I parked and walked towards the heavy wooden double doors, dwarfed by their size. Up close, disturbing details emerged—grotesques carved into the arches, stained-glass portraits of tortured figures. I actually considered turning around right then.

But I summoned my nerves and pulled on the rusted iron handle. The door's groan echoed through the silent grounds. I stepped into the dim, musty interior that smelled of age and disuse.

Two severe-looking older people dressed in drab clothing stood in the foyer waiting. Their body language made it clear this was not a warmly welcoming place.

"Dr. Rawlins, I presume?" the withered man said in a dry tone. "We are the Keepers. This way."

With that, they turned and strode down the corridor without another word. I had to jog to keep up as they showed me around in eerie silence.

The Manor's interior was just as unsettling—shadows looming in every corner, chipped paint, sagging ceilings, and cobwebs galore. It felt like the grounds' decay had seeped inside over centuries of abandonment.

What struck me most was the distinct lack of people. They led me through deserted lounge areas, a library, and even recreational rooms. We passed two or three people in white robes who stopped and stared vacantly. Were those the patients?

After the tour, the Keepers sat me down in a parlor. "You seem a… willful sort," the woman said, eyeing me with obvious disdain. "Grimmwood requires dedication and strength."

As they grilled me on my qualifications, a clear tension oozed between them. Their dynamic was so cold, almost adversarial. Were these two even together or kept hostage by the roles of Keepers?

When they finished, I sensed they were not impressed by me at all. But to my surprise, they offered me the psychiatrist position on the spot. Something desperation in their dour demeanor made it impossible to refuse.

Just as the oppressive interview was finally ending, the parlor door creaked open. In stepped another person - a man around my age, though his demeanor made him seem more weathered.

"Ah, Dr. Blake," the male Keeper said flatly. "This is Dr. Emily Rawlins, your potential new…colleague."

The man called Dr. Blake gave me a slow once-over, his intense, piercing eyes making me squirm a bit. He was quite handsome in a rugged way, with tousled dark hair and chiseled features. But something about him seemed almost feral, unkempt.

"Colleague, hmm?" His voice was low and gravelly. "We'll see about that."

Dr. Blake sauntered over, hands jammed in his pockets. His clothes looked slept-in, his shirt untucked. He carried an aura of just not caring what anyone thought.

Up close, his presence was simultaneously unsettling yet…magnetic. I couldn't decide if I was intrigued or wanted to run away.

"So, Dr. Rawlins," he said, eyes boring into me. "A fresh young shrink looking to join our merry little asylum. What makes you think you can hack it here?"

His blunt challenge knocked me off guard. "I…I have excellent credentials and experience helping patients with a variety of mental health issues."

Dr. Blake let out a gruff chuckle. "You have no idea what you're in for. The patients here, their issues…let's just say they go beyond your textbook definitions of sanity."

I bristled a bit at his condescending tone. Who did this disheveled man think he was?

"With all due respect, Dr. Blake, I'm more than capable of handling challenging cases. Perhaps you'd prefer I don't tread on your territory?"

Our eyes locked in a simmering staredown. His lips curled in an arrogant smirk.

"On the contrary. I welcome the chance to watch you crack under pressure. Few make it at Grimmwood for long."

The tension increased to another level. Part of me wanted to wipe that smug look off his face. Yet…I also felt an unmistakable spark, an animal magnetism. This man got under my skin, but not entirely in an unpleasant way.

The way he leaned in close, the musky scent of his cologne surrounding me, it was unnerving yet intoxicating at the same time.

"That's enough, Blake," the female Keeper snapped, shattering the charged moment. "Dr. Rawlins has accepted the position. You're to give her your full…cooperation, is that clear?"

Dr. Blake held my stare a beat longer before shrugging nonchalantly.

"Crystal," he said, already turning to exit. "Looking forward to working together, Doctor."

His tone dripped with insinuation that stretched far beyond professional courtesy. A shiver ran through me as the door clicked shut behind him.

The Keepers then turned to me, their dour expressions saying they noticed the tension too. Some unspoken communication passed between the old duo before the man spoke up.

"Well then. Welcome to Grimmwood Manor, Dr. Rawlins. We'll get the paperwork processed right away…"

As I gave a hesitant nod and forced a polite smile, my mind was still stuck on Dr. Ethan Blake. Just who was this man who could rattle me so? Was hiring at this isolated place really a good idea after all?

Yet despite all the alarm bells, that thrill of danger mixed with undeniable attraction had me totally disarmed. Like it or not, it seemed the roguish doctor was about to loom large in my life from now on.

It was really happening. After giving notice at the hospital and packing up my dingy apartment, I said farewell to the noise and grime of the city. I loaded up my car and began the long drive to my new life at Grimmwood Manor.

The trip felt like slowly being separated from the familiar world. Towering skyscrapers gave way to trees stretching endlessly in every direction. Traffic congestion faded to the hum of nature. I could breathe again without the weight of urban smog.

As I pulled up the winding drive to the manor, it loomed more ominously than before. The sun was just setting, casting long shadows from theforest that seemed to be closing in around the building and grounds.

I grabbed my bags from the trunk and tentatively approached the main doors. They were slightly ajar, creaking in the evening breeze. The musty, decaying scent of the interior wafted out, making me pause.

Was I really going to just move into this foreboding place alone? Abandon the safety and comforts I knew? A raven's harsh caw from a nearby tree made me jump. This wildness was going to take some getting used to.

But I plowed ahead and stepped over the threshold, determined to embrace this fresh start no matter what. A wizened old woman in a white robe silently appeared to lead me to the staff quarters.

My new living space was somewhat rudimentary—a simple bedroom, bathroom, and sitting area with scratched wood floors and cracked walls. The old lady didn't utter a single word before shuffling away, leaving me alone amid the eerie silence.

With my few belongings, I made the sparse quarters as cozy as possible. Some scented candles, soft blankets, and framed photos helped give it a relaxing feel.

But just as I put the final touches in place, reality set in. A guttural groaning seemed to rise up from the surrounding black woods, the trees creaking in an ominous rhythm. Then a piercing howl echoed in the distance, raising the hairs on my arms.

What had I gotten myself into, leaving civilization behind completely? This felt less like a healing retreat and more like being consumed by dark, primal wilderness.

A sharp tapping at the bedroom window made me nearly jump out of my skin. I whipped around to see a raven's beady eyes peering in like an omen of what awaited me here. Its clawed feet scratched the glass as it beckoned me into the night.

My heart pounding, I moved to the window and stared out at the ancient forest enshrouding the manor. Twisted branches clawed at the starry sky while the pained groans grew louder all around me.

Yet at that moment, despite all the unsettling wildness pressing in, I felt a profound sense of freedom—of escaping the real cage—the concrete labyrinth of the city. Here, maybe I could finally breathe and find some semblance of peace and purpose again.

I closed my eyes, basked in the cool night air, and let the sounds of untamed nature wrap around me. Whatever dark secrets this place harbored, I was ready to face them. This was my rebirth.

CHAPTER TWO

2

FIRST PATIENTS

The morning light filtering through the trees felt eerie, almost sickly. But I tried to shake off the unsettling vibes as I headed to the manor's main entrance for my first official day on the job at Grimmwood.

The heavy wooden doors groaned open to reveal the gloomy foyer. The two dour Keepers stood waiting, their perpetual scowls ingrained on their wrinkled faces. Without so much as a "good morning," they launched into my orientation.

With clipped tones, they led me on a brisk tour of the areas I'd be working —the nurses' station, my private office space, and the common rooms for sessions. Everywhere we went, the place was draped in shadows and thick cobwebs, like it was stuck in an endless state of decay.

"There are currently fourteen patients residing here," the male Keeper stated flatly. "You'll be assigned nine for individual therapy sessions and oversee their treatment plans."

The female Keeper shot me a piercing look. "I trust you were adequately prepared during your studies for…unique psychological cases?"

Before I could respond, her partner continued, "The minds you'll be tending to here have ventured to dark places. You would be wise to keep an open one."

With that ominous warning, the Keepers abruptly departed, leaving me alone in the dingy office amid stale stacks of files on my desk. So much for any sort of real training or support.

I set about unpacking my supplies and attempting to make the depressing space my own. But my unease grew as I fastened my diploma to the wall alongside disturbing artistic prints - figures contorted in human misery. Just what had I signed myself up for here?

Pushing my doubt aside, I took a steadying breath and officially opened my appointment book. A parade of unfamiliar names for the day's patients greeted me.

With the Keepers' words lingering heavily in the air, I prepared to dive headfirst into the "unique" minds awaiting me at Grimmwood Manor. If only I realized then just how dark the waters would become.

A soft knock at the office door made me jump. I took a calming breath and called out, "Come in."

The door creaked open, and a young woman meekly entered. She couldn't have been more than 25, with a fragile, haunted look about her. This must be my first patient, Laura Weston.

"H-hello Dr. Rawlins," she said in a small voice, hugging her arms tight. "It's nice to meet you."

I gave her what I hoped was a reassuring smile. "Nice to meet you too, Laura. Please, have a seat and make yourself comfortable."

Laura tucked a loose strand of hair behind her ear and settled into the chair across from my desk. Even with her attempts at politeness, she looked absolutely terrified.

"Th-they told me you'd be taking over my case," she stammered. "I want you to know I'm not…I'm not making this up or crazy, I swear."

I leaned forward with an open expression. "Laura, I believe you completely. Why don't you tell me what's been happening in your own words?"

She took a shaky breath and began. "For the past six months, I've been having this recurring nightmare that feels so real, like I'm actually living through it…"

Laura proceeded to describe an absolutely horrific series of dream images. Of being alone in a pitch-black forest, branches clawing at her from all sides. The sounds of feral snarls echo from the darkness as she runs blindly, terrified.

Then her dream self comes face-to-face with…itself. Another version of Laura, eyes black as night, jaws unhinged in a fanged rictus, her own reflection distorted into a demonic, unholy fiend.

"It's like staring into a twisted, evil mirror," she said, eyes brimming with tears. The creature…it knows everything about me—my fears, my hopes, my darkest secrets. And it wants to consume me, make me one with it forever."

As Laura graphically depicted being mercilessly pursued by this vile doppelganger, I felt a chill run down my spine. This was beyond any normal night terror.

"I-I wake up screaming, shaking, with awful scratches all over that I can't explain," she whimpered, pushing up her sleeve to reveal deep gouges crisscrossing her pale forearm. "It's like the nightmare follows me out, bleeding into reality…"

Laura dissolved into heartbroken sobs then, face in her hands. I sat in stunned silence, horrifically transfixed by her depiction yet utterly unequipped to process it. If this was just my first patient meeting, god help me with what other fresh nightmares awaited.

After my jarring session with Laura, I barely had a chance to collect myself before my next patient arrived. This time it was an elderly man, somewhere in his 70s, who entered with a cane and a soft, distant look in his eyes.

"Good day, Dr. Rawlins," he said in a wispy voice as he slowly lowered himself into the chair. I'm Harold Edmunds, though I expect you're already familiar with my condition."

I offered a gentle smile, trying not to look as shaken as I felt. "It's very nice to meet you, Harold. Please, tell me about what you've been experiencing."

Harold gave a solemn nod and began recounting his issues in a frail yet resolute tone. His nightmare, while not as overtly horrific as Laura's, still chilled me to the bone.

"Every night, without fail, I find myself pulled into the same haunting dream. I'm standing in the woods just outside the manor grounds. The trees loom in around me, gnarled and ominous even in my unconscious state."

He paused, his rheumy eyes looking past me out the window at those woods in the distance. I repressed a shudder, motioning for him to continue.

"As I make my way through the darkness, a faint light appears through the twisted branches. That's when I first glimpse the lake - its black waters utterly still yet seeming to shiver with barely contained dread."

Harold fell silent again, jaw tensing as he relieved it. I found myself leaning forward, rapt.

"And that's when I see her," he whispered hoarsely. "Elizabeth, my dearest wife who passed twelve years ago. She's there, standing atop that ominous lake as if born anew from its unholy depths."

Tears welled up in the old man's eyes, but he refused to let them fall. "No matter how loudly I call out to her, beg for her to return to me, she cannot hear. Her ghostly form simply turns and beckons for me to join her out across those stagnant waters."

Harold's withered hands clenched his cane until the knuckles whitened. "I run towards the shore, stumbling, praying to reach her before she fades away again. But no matter how hard I try, the lake's edge remains just out of grasp each time I awake in a cold sweat."

He looked up at me, eyes haunted. "That nightmare plagues me every single night, growing more vivid and desperate over time. I fear soon the dark waters will finally claim me, to whatever twisted fate awaits on the other side."

Exhaling a shuddered breath, I sat in stunned silence. My professional assurances and explanations utterly failed me at that moment. Harold's living torment, like Laura's, hinted at something far more sinister and unnatural, twisting this manor's reality. I felt ill-prepared for what lay ahead.

Over the following days, I saw patient after patient, each describing progressively more disturbing dream experiences. At first, I tried to find logical patterns and explanations based on my psychiatric training. But the more I heard, the more my grasp on reality seemed to loosen.

Sue, a middle-aged woman, spoke of endless night visions of being buried alive, soil filling her lungs as she clawed helplessly at the coffin walls. Jake, a teenage boy, recounted graphic terrors of his own body mutating and disfiguring before his eyes in grotesque ways.

Despite their differing ages, genders, and backgrounds, the narratives all followed a similar dark, malevolent undercurrent. Shadowy dimensions are just adjacent to our own plane of existence. Dreamworlds that refused to remain separate from the waking one. Descriptions of truly unholy, indescribable forces preying upon their psyches.

I tried my usual therapeutic techniques - cognitive reframing, coping exercises, and even exploring potential metaphors their subconscious could be expressing. But nothing seemed to override or rationalize the visceral terror each patient exhibited. This went beyond mere bad dreams or psychological abstracts.

"I know how this sounds," one patient, an older woman named Agatha, had said in a trembling rasp. "But mark my words, that ungodly presence is coming for us all. It wants to shred the veil completely and drag us all screaming into its maw of eternal anguish!"

Agatha's wild-eyed raving, her gnarled hands clawing the air, should have prompted professional detachment and intervention from me. Instead, a creeping sense of dread wormed its way into my very core that day, hard as I tried to repress it.

What malign forces could be causing these shared experiences of existential, apocalyptic dread across the entire patient population? My academic frameworks felt hopelessly insufficient, mere fairy tales compared to whatever primordial evil was gestating here.

I found myself questioning everything - my own sanity, even the nature of reality itself as I knew it. Grimmwood's isolation now felt increasingly oppressive, the shadows and gnarled groves surrounding us more ominous by the day. If I stayed on this path, where might it ultimately lead?

As the nightmare cases continued to pile up with eerily similar threads, I knew I needed to confide my growing concerns in someone. Despite our heated first meeting, Dr. Blake was the only one who seemed even remotely willing to engage.

I caught up with him in one of the manor's dusty common rooms, where he was kicking back with a leatherbound book. He glanced up as I entered, one eyebrow raised.

'Well, if it isn't the rookie shrink," he drawled. "Let me guess - the patients' dream demons are proving too much for you already?"

I steeled myself against his mocking tone. "Actually, I wanted to run something by you. I'm seeing…patterns in the nightmare cases. Shared images, forces, landscapes. It goes beyond just individual subconscious fears."

Blake snapped his book shut, giving me his full, disinterested attention with a lazy spin of one hand. "Do go on, Dr. Rawlins. Enlighten me with your clearing insight mere weeks in."

Ignoring his sarcasm, I launched into explicit details I'd heard—the gnarled, sinister woods, the blurring of dream and reality, the sense of some infinite malice lurking just out of sight, hungering to break through completely.

To his credit, Blake's cocky smirk gradually faded the more I piled on the visceral examples. He unconsciously leaned forward, eyes narrowing.

"You pick up on those underlying patterns a bit too eagerly for my liking," he said, measuring tone replacing his former nonchalance. "Best to let well enough alone with that nonsense."

I shook my head firmly. "But that's just it - this goes beyond mere nightmares or psychoses! I've never seen or read about anything like the collective experiences described here. If they're all being somehow...influenced by the same forces, don't we have a responsibility to get to the heart of it?"

Blake rose to his feet, and all traces of humor vanished from his chiseled features. He closed the distance between us with a few long strides, eyes boring into mine with startling intensity.

"Listen very closely, Emily," he said in a low, weighty timbre. "There are some depths here you do not want to plumb, no matter how curious. For both our sakes, I suggest you heed my advice - steer clear of that line of questioning before it's too late."

A shiver ran through me then, not born of fear but rather something else lurking beneath the doctor's stark warning. This wasn't mere posturing or existential dread.

He knew something, had seen something, that convinced him some була remained best unexplored and unspoken of at Grimmwood Manor. And part of me couldn't help but be intrigued to discover what that was.

That night, despite my exhaustion, my mind refused to rest. Dr. Blake's ominous warnings replayed on a loop, mingling with the unsettling stories from my newly acquired patients. Were darker forces truly at work here, or was I merely getting caught up in the collective mania?

Finally, sometime after midnight, an unease-filled slumber found me. But there was no respite to be had, as my subconscious quickly betrayed me...

I found myself standing in the manor's gloomy foyer, though the shadows seemed exponentially deeper, more pervasive. An unnatural, oppressive silence hung in the air, suffocating.

Suddenly, a thick, dripping sound made me flinch. Craning my neck, I saw a black viscous ooze beginning to seep downwards from the darkness, overwhelming the ceiling above.

The vile flow quickened, compounding into a torrent of wretched ichor that defied gravity. My gaze pulled upwards against my will, following the pulsating stream to its unholy source.

There, breaching through an unseen cosmic chasm where the ceiling should have been, a titanic, fanged maw emerged from the roiling ooze. Endless rows of hooked, serrated teeth, attached to...nothing, simply an abyss of bristling hunger.

The gaping, lightless void seemed to swell, growing impossibly larger, while the deluge of putrescence poured down in greater volume. I watched in revulsed horror as the ravenous maw began devouring the staircase I was rooted upon, dragging it upwards into its ragged gullet.

I scrambled backward, feeling the inexorable pull towards that infinite, lightless oblivion waiting with gnashing jaws to swallow me whole. The dank, septic odor of the ooze overwhelmed me as it closed in from all sides, leaving no escape.

Suffocating, drowning in sheer mortal dread, I reached the top step only to stare straight into the lipless, fanged yaw. Icy tendrils of despair slithered forth, coiling around my soul as I was helplessly drawn inward to be devoured

That's when I startled awake, bolt upright with a strangled cry. My heart thundered as I gasped for air, clammy sweat drenching me. Gulping down precious reality, I instinctively cast a horrified look out the bedroom window.

The gnarled trees outside appeared to lean inward, their crooked shadows clawing against the glass, hungering. At that moment, I couldn't help but wonder what sort of unspeakable evil lurking within the boundaries of Grimmwood Manor itself.

3

The Manor's History

I jolted awake, my heart pounding like a drum in my ears. Sweat drenched my sheets and nightgown as I sucked in ragged breaths. For a few disorienting moments, I couldn't tell what was reality and what was the remnants of that demonic nightmare.

Gulping down air, I gazed around my modest bedroom, allowing its sparse familiarity to anchor me slowly. The gnarled tree branches scratched at the window. The flickering candles cast dancing shadows—all as it should be in my little sanctuary at Grimmwood Manor.

Except nothing felt right or safe anymore.

Those vile dream images clung to the corners of my mind like tar - the fanged, endless maw devouring the staircase, viscous ooze oozing from unseen depths to swallow me whole. It all felt so lucid, so inescapably real in the moment.

And maybe that's what disturbed me most. If my subconscious could conjure up such grotesquely twisted realms, what did that say about the state of my psyche? Or was there something more…influential at play here, seeping into my slumber?

The thought of those infernal nightmares besieging the manor's patients resurfaced. Their tormented descriptions now carried infinitely more weight after encountering a mere glimpse of myself. We were all being exposed to the same unholy, innominate forces, whether awake or asleep.

A cold determination washed over me then. I couldn't sit idly by, grasping at academic straws while something ancient and insidious took root inside these very walls. Not when the solution may lay buried amid the cobwebbed recesses of this place's undoubtedly sordid history.

Throwing aside the covers, I quickly dressed and strode with purpose out into the shadowy corridors. Snaking through the gloomy path burned into my memory, I arrived at the heavy door leading to the neglected records room.

The air hung stale and musty like few had disturbed this tomb in generations. My fingers trailed the dust outlining old cabinets and shelves stuffed to bursting with ancient, unlabeled ledgers and journals. So many secrets left to entomb, discarded from human memory.

But I would unearth them. I would dig up every last shred of this decrepit institution's transgressions if that's what it took to shed light on the nightmare currently engulfing us all. Inhaling the cloying scent of disturbed decay, my search began in earnest.

After sifting through stacks of decaying files and ledgers, a clear picture finally emerged of Grimmwood's sordid origins. This manor was built in the late 1800s as a psychiatric hospital called Grimmwood Sanatorium. But it was no ordinary mental institution.

The more I discovered about their "treatment" methods, the more disturbed I became. Grimmwood employed unorthodox, torturous techniques that made my skin crawl. Rusted restraints and straitjackets for "violent" patients. Actual surgical tools for performing barbaric procedures like the crude lobotomies of the era. Rows of tiny padded cells they called "Enlightenment Rooms" for sensory deprivation.

Jotted notes and disturbing illustrations showed just how sadistic this place was. Patients strapped to tables, drooling and mutilated. Orderlies in ghoulish masks performing experimental shock treatments and injections with unknown substances. The whole sanatorium seemed engineered to break people's minds rather than heal them.

But perhaps most chilling were the plentiful records of patients suffering 'Night Sickness" - a term used to describe their agonizing, relentless bouts of night terrors and delirium.

Page after page contained haunting firsthand accounts of the dreaming torments. Visions of shadowy demon creatures tormenting them for hours on end, both asleep and awake. Lucid nightmares where the boundaries between reality and their personal hells blurred completely. Some even spoke of their individual terror realms "merging" with other patients in a vast, infinite abyss of fear.

The more drastic and cruel Grimmwood's remedies became, the more the Night Sickness seemed to mutate wildly out of control. Doubling down on radical deprivations and brain surgeries only spawned waking hallucinations of entire cabals conjuring dark entities. Entire wards became overrun by mass psychogenic delusions and violence on a corporal scale.

It was as if these archaic, misguided methods were actually amplifying the very night terrors they aimed to extinguish. They had stumbled upon some obscene metaphysical barrier they were never meant to breach, proceeding only to rip open a wider, horrific dimension beyond human comprehension to pour through.

I sat back feeling shaken, the heavy old records casting deeper and deeper palls of gloom over my soul. The Grimmwood of the 19th century sounded less like a hospital and more like the burial grounds of the damned. Something wicked had indelibly stained these halls, and now it seemed resurgent, fueled by reopening the facility's dormant foundations.

Buried beneath piles of crumbling files, a particular aged leather book made my heart skip a beat - the private journal of Dr. Solomon Harding himself. The man whose barbaric methods had driven Grimmwood Sanatorium into a waking nightmare.

With a deep breath to steady my nerves, I pulled open the weathered cover shattering the silence of the archives. Harding's tight, erratic scrawl leaped off the first few pages like the ravings of a brilliant mind teetering on the edge of madness:

"The night terrors that plague our residents are no mere affliction but a tantalizing window into the disparate reality lurking beneath our own fragile plane of existence. If I can only pry that crevice wider…"

From these preliminaries, it became grotesquely clear that Harding had progressed far beyond the clinical study of bad dreams. He'd become dangerously preoccupied with the notion of an entire dimension coalescing from the darker recesses of the human subconscious.

He termed this infinite abyss of formless fear "The Obscuratus"—an oozing, spectral underbelly giving birth to the very night monsters manifesting in our nightmares. In Harding's words, it is a "tenebrous and unknowable dimension in reverse, where our phobias and neuroses are made corporeal as chattering shades bent on their own virulent propagation."

Page after page, I watched the brilliant director's determination curve into a twisted obsession with breaching the Obscuratus at all costs. His methods for treating the Sanatorium's patients grew only more unhinged as he pressed the boundaries of those dreaming thresholds.

Arcane formulae and demented diagrams filled the journal's gutters, hinting at blasphemous rituals constructed to forcibly invite the nightmare realm's spectral hostilities. Harding's handwriting degenerated into frenzied scribbles, torn between solemn rapture at glimpsing the Obscuratum's periphery and blind terror at what untold forces were pulling on the other side.

Then, one final, chilling entry dated over a century ago:

"At long last, my work takes its final, feverish turn! This night, through the blackest of rites, I shall at last pass beyond the shroud of sleep entirely and take dominion over the negatively refracting animosities of the Dread Obscuratum.

While this may very well consume what pitiable remnants of my mortal essence remain, the choice has long been made. By shattering the veiled frontier between our worlds, I ascend as a harbinger of a new age of revelation, ushering humanity's enlightened transcendence by fire!"

The rest of the journal's pages were viciously scratched out or torn away completely. A cold sweat prickled my brow as I stared at those final feverish scrawls, feeling almost relieved that whatever blasphemy Harding invoked remained inscrutable.

Yet a gnawing disquiet embedded itself deep within me too. If that madman had indeed succeeded in prizing open a rift to the dread Obscuratum, what unfathomable consequences might still echo through these accursed halls over a hundred years later?

As those shadowed archival stacks seemed to leer with fresh menace, I couldn't escape the sense that Grimmwood's sordid history was merely a prelude to something far more disquieting awakening once again.

After poring over Dr. Harding's final, unhinged journal entries, the inevitable coverup and whitewashing became painfully clear. Whatever profane rites the madman carried out in his obsession with the "Obscuratum," the results were nothing short of catastrophic.

Tucked amid the scattered reports and press clippings, I found documentation of a full-blown panic surrounding Grimmwood in the days following Harding's disappearance. Whispers and allegations of patients being tormented by "unholy night terrors" and "waking visions of malevolent specters" began leaking out.

Harrowing firsthand accounts told of entire wards descending into mass psychosis and violence, overrun by shared delusions of dark forces breaching into reality itself. Some reports cryptically referred to "cosmic bellows" and "luminous rifts" opening within the very grounds of Grimmwood.

Whatever Harding had unleashed in his pursuit of the Obscuratum, it bled rampantly into the waking world in a sordid display of psychogenic horror. The sanatorium's parent company and state overseers were forced to step in and shutter the entire facility in utter disgrace.

All records, materials, and testimony relating to those final blasphemous days were seemingly buried or destroyed to cover up the scandal. Grimmwood itself was rapidly sealed off, left to sit rotting as an abandoned monument to institutional hubris and the wages of prying too greedily into unknowable dimensions.

For over a century, the dilapidated buildings and sloping grounds were a gravestone deformity on the rural hillside - shunned by the fearful locals and reclaimed by the overgrown forests gradually enshrouding it. Whatever malignant aura still clung to the site like a curse was simply left to fester, allowed to decay into faded history.

That is, until some ill-fated real estate conglomerate purchased the land for a paltry sum recently, eager to reverse-renovate the husk into a chic "psychological retreat" at rock-bottom overhead. The sins and depravities committed at Grimmwood were swept aside as easily as clearing the cobwebs, dismissed as archaic superstitions unfit for enlightened modern times.

As I pieced together the systematic sanitization of Grimmwood's wretched past, I felt a cold anger harden inside me. All those lives shattered, indelible traumas inflicted - simply papered over through corporate avarice and society's own willful amnesia. Just waiting to be unearthed once again, messily and without remorse, by whatever ancient evil still festered here.

I was so engrossed in the disturbing historical accounts that the records room door slamming open made me practically jump out of my skin. Dr. Blake stood there, eyes blazing with fury.

"Just what in the hell do you think you're doing, Rawlins?" he growled, storming over to where I sat surrounded by the ancient files.

I instinctively shrank back as he loomed over me, radiating volatile anger. "I...I was just researching some background on this place to better understand-"

"You're dredging up things better left buried. That's what you're doing!" Blake's raised voice echoed harshly through the archives. "Grimmwood's history is a cesspool you don't want any part of, believe me."

Meeting his scorching glare, I felt my own resolve harden. "With all due respect, I'm seeing clear patterns in the patients' night terrors that indicate some very real, very malignant forces at work here."

I held up the weathered journal for emphasis. "These records speak of rituals that may have opened some kind of horrific portal or dimension…one that still seems to be lingering, seeping into our reality."

Blake's nostrils flared as I challenged his stark dismissals. His rough hand snatched the book from my grasp as he flipped through its scribbled pages furiously.

"You're treading on the ground way out of your league," he seethed in a low, dangerous tone. "That raving lunatic's writings are the product of a mind utterly divorced from reason or ethics. Just the very thing we're supposed to be helping people escape from!"

I shook my head adamantly, unmoved. "Then why are so many of the patients describing the exact same gateways to fear, the same infinite dimensions of terror? It can't just be random delusions!"

Blake reared back, eyes wide as a cornered animal. For a tortured moment, it seemed like he might lash out physically. But instead, he slammed the journal down with a deafening bang, face contorted in a rictus sneer.

"You want to keep digging into Pandora's vortex. That's your risk. But don't say I didn't warn you, Emily." He leaned in so close I could smell the whiskey on his breath. "You're opening doors that must remain closed at all costs, even if we have to bury them beneath this goddamn hill ourselves!"

With that, he turned and stormed away, leaving me shaken. Blake's outburst hinted he harbored deeper, darker knowledge about the true nature of the forces we were up against here.

And despite his vehement protests, it only convinced me further that I was onto something too dreadfully vital to ignore, no matter where it led. For all our sakes, I had to see this through - no matter what Stygian thresholds awaited.

That night, any hopes I had of finding peaceful sleep were shattered by shrill screams piercing the manor's eerie quiet. I jolted awake to the sounds of pure pandemonium erupting from the residential halls.

Throwing on a robe, I rushed out into the dimly lit corridor where the commotion was growing - a cavalcade of terrified shrieks, thunderous crashes, and the unmistakable snarls of feral rage.

By the time I reached the source, a scene of abject chaos assaulted me. Cowering staffers pressed against the walls as a heavyset middle-aged man - one of our patients - raged in the middle of the hall, upending furniture and slamming his body against the walls.

He wasn't just having a night terror. He had become one.

Wild-eyed and frothing, the man's massive frame seemed seized by an unseen, violent force. Powerful orderlies in surgical garb tried frantically to restrain his thrashing limbs, but not before several took vicious blows that left them bleeding.

Unfurling from his mouth was a nonstop, guttural bellowing that raised the hairs on my arms - a primordial tongue ripping from his very core, giving an animalistic voice to some ancient, encroaching darkness.

"It consumes! It consumes!" he howled in a tongue uglier than any human language as I watched in shaken revulsion. "Kalahrízō opens the path! We are ended needed!"

One of the brutes managed to finally sedate and wrangle the raving man into ruthless restraints. But even as they carried his deadweight form away, those unseeing eyes still burned straight through me, beckoning the void with each rasping breath.

In them, I saw the same lurking malevolence that had haunted my latest nightmare, yawning endlessly behind the thin veneer of our workaday reality. That same existential dread, given gnashing, lupine form.

If there was any doubt that the patients were all being preyed upon by the same coalescing forces from the Obscuratum, it was permanently extinguished. My obsession had been more than validated—those ancient, unholy seals had been irrevocably breached, and the darkness was pouring through in earnest.

Trembling, I steeled myself to the harshest truth. Whatever intangible terror Dr. Harding had woken up all those years ago, it had clearly never left these grounds. And unless I found the courage to shatter its hold permanently, the nightmare would stretch on, consuming us all without relenting.

CHAPTER 4

31

4

Romantic Entanglement

From the moment Dr. Blake arrived at Grimmwood Manor, I felt a spark between us. He was so charming and confident, with a warm smile and twinkle in his eye. Whenever we were in the same room, I couldn't help but sneak glances his way. My heart would flutter just a little bit faster when he spoke.

At first, I tried to brush it off as simply being excited to work with someone so accomplished in our field. But I knew, deep down, there was an undeniable physical attraction simmering under the surface. The way he carried himself, the sound of his voice, and even just his presence made my head spin dizzily. I felt giddy, like a schoolgirl with a crush.

Our flirtatious banter started off seemingly innocent - shared jokes, lingering eye contact, casual touches on the arm or back. But it quickly escalated into something more charged, more heated. The sexual tension was palpable whenever we were alone together.

The other staff took notice, too. I could feel their judgmental stares whenever Dr. Blake and I engaged in one of our flirty exchanges. Hushed whispers and sideways glances made it clear they felt we were being inappropriate and unprofessional. A couple of nurses even mustered the audacity to confront me about keeping things professional with my colleague.

I knew they were right that getting entangled with a coworker crossed lines. But the spark between Dr. Blake and I just kept smoldering hotter and hotter until it felt like an inevitability that it would erupt into flames.

It nearly did one day when we were reviewing a patient file together. Pouring over the details of their disturbing nightmares, Dr. Blake leaned in close beside me. Our bodies were nearly touching, the heat radiating between us. I could smell his intoxicating cologne. When he put his hand on my arm to underscore a point, I nearly melted at his touch. At that moment, I felt an overwhelming urge to pull him against me and kiss him deeply…

I was poring over the old files again late one night, trying to unravel the secrets of Grimmwood Manor's sordid past. The dim lamp on my desk cast an eerie glow as I examined disturbing reports of experimental treatments and rumored occult practices from decades prior. A chill ran down my spine at the macabre details.

Suddenly, the creak of a door broke the silence. I spun around to see Dr. Blake standing in the doorway, a rakish grin spread across his face. My heart started pounding in my chest as his eyes raked over me hungrily.

"Burning the midnight oil, I see," he purred in that rich baritone voice that always made me go weak in the knees. Blake sauntered towards me with a predatory stride. I could smell his intoxicating cologne wafting closer with every step.

"I…I was just catching up on some research," I stammered, flustered by his mere presence. He was standing so close now that I could feel the warmth radiating from his body.

"You work too hard," Blake murmured huskily. "You need to learn to unwind take a break…" His fingers traced along my arm, raising goosebumps.

I stifled a shudder at his scorching touch. Part of me knew I should pull away and remain professional. But the gravitational pull between us was too strong to resist. My willpower melted away as Blake leaned in closer, his lips hovering agonizingly close to mine.

The next moment, we were locked in a searing embrace, our mouths devouring each other in ravenous need. His muscular arms enveloped me as I clung to him desperately. We stumbled backward, strewing papers across the desk as Blake urgently lifted me onto it without breaking our passionate kiss.

Our bodies pressed flush, I could feel the hardness of his desire straining against me. A tingling heat bloomed between my legs as his hands roamed feverishly over my curves. Gasping into his mouth, I feverishly tore at his shirt while he hiked up my skirt…

In the hazy afterglow, I rested my head on Dr. Blake's chest, our bodies still intertwined and slick with sweat. His strong arms encircled me as we lay tangled together, savoring the intimate moment. I traced lazy patterns across the chiseled contours of his torso, feeling completely at ease.

"Blake," I murmured against his skin. "Can I confide something in you?" He planted a tender kiss on my forehead, urging me to continue.

I took a deep breath before divulging the fears that had been gnawing at me. "It's about the patients' nightmares. I…I think there may be something more sinister linking them together."

He stiffened slightly beside me, but I pressed on. "The dream narratives, the details, the similarities - it's too coincidental. I've been looking into Grimmwood's history and found some...disturbing things." I recounted my findings about repressed records of unorthodox treatments and whispers of the occult.

As I spoke, Blake's body tensed even more. When I finally fell silent, I glanced up at his face and felt a stab of cold dread pierce my heart. Gone was the warm, passionate expression from moments before. Now, his features were hardened into a mask of barely contained disquiet, and...was that anger flickering in his eyes?

"You're letting your imagination run away with you," he said in a clipped tone, abruptly pushing me away. "They're just dreams, for God's sake. You're obsessing over nothing."

I recoiled at his stern dismissal, feeling a confusing swirl of hurt, disbelief, and rising ire. "But the evidence - the records I found..."

Blake silenced me with a glare. "You're a doctor, not a historian. Leave the past alone and focus on your real job - helping your current patients improve." His words carried an unmistakable note of censure, triggering doubts in my mind.

As he rose from the bed without a backward glance, I wrapped the sheets around my naked body, suddenly feeling cold and small. What had only minutes ago been a scene of intimate connection was now pervaded by a chilling awkwardness and sense that something wasn't quite right.

I watched Blake gather his clothes, his movements brisk and aloof. When he paused in the doorway, I thought he might say something to ameliorate the growing rift. Instead, he simply shot me a bemused look and left without another word.

I sat there, reeling from a maelstrom of conflicting emotions that left me second-guessing everything—my discoveries, my suspicions, my relationship with this man I realized I hardly knew at all. An ominous sense of dread began creeping over me, leaving me wondering what—or who—I had somehow gotten inextricably entangled with.

In the days following my intimate night with Dr. Blake, I found my mind consumed with doubts and a growing fixation on the patients' plights. Our passionate tryst had been quickly overshadowed by the disturbing conversation that followed. Try as I might to push it aside, I couldn't let go of the nagging feeling that something wasn't right at Grimmwood Manor.

Blake, for his part, seemed intent on avoiding me outside of mandatory staff meetings. Whenever our paths crossed in the halls or counseling rooms, he would shoot me curt looks laced with irritation before brushing past. The warm rapport we once shared had turned icy cold. I yearned to rekindle the intimacy, to regain the closeness I had briefly tasted. But he made it abundantly clear his focus was strictly professional now.

My obsession with uncovering the truth, however, only intensified. At night my dreams grew more and more disturbing - horrific visions of the patients' terrifying nightmares as if I were living them myself. I would wake up in a cold sweat, replaying the graphic images over and over in my mind. Twisted monstrosities and shrouded figures plagued my sleep and exhausted me during the day.

During my waking hours, I pored over every patient file, scouring the transcripts of their nightmare narratives, looking for patterns or connecting threads. The more I read, the more unnerved I became at the unmistakable similarities in the dreams—dark entities infiltrating the subconscious, tor- turous mindscapes, an underlying current of ancient malice. I knew I wasn't imagining things. My instincts screamed that something truly evil was at work.

Part of me wondered if I shouldn't simply pursue the spark I felt with Blake, to hell with probing into Grimmwood's shady past. Life could be so much simpler that way - his arms around me again, our bodies intertwined with searing passion, losing myself in his smoldering gaze.

But each night, the disturbing visions would return, haunting my sleep and strengthening my resolve. I owed it to these tortured patients to not give up, to unearth whatever diabolical forces preyed upon their unconscious minds. A heaping portion of guilt weighed on me that I may have led them into this nightmare unknowingly by accepting the job here.

So, despite the confusing mix of desire, fear, and obsession warring within me, I knew I had to stay focused on seeking answers. Blake and our sizzling chemistry would have to be put on indefinite hold. For now, my priority was shining a light into the grim shadows that seemed to be swallowing us all at Grimmwood - before it was too late.

5

Descent Into Madness

As I made my evening rounds, a growing knot of dread twisted my stomach tighter with each patient report. The night terrors seemed to worsen, intensifying into something far beyond normal dreams. I could hear the panic and horror in their voices as they recounted the latest visions tormenting their sleep.

"Clawed shadows devouring my soul…"
"Faceless specters dragging me into the abyss…"
"A dark bramble consuming all light and hope…"

The disturbing imagery filled my mind, making my heart race with visceral fear and anxiety. What unholy forces were visiting such disturbing torment upon these poor souls? My research raised more unsettling questions by the day.

Finally, I arrived at John Sawyer's room. A longtime resident, he had been one of the most severely afflicted by the nightmares. I steeled myself before entering, unsure of what anguished state I would find him in.

The dim lights cast eerie shadows across his trembling form. Sawyer rocked back and forth frantically on the edge of his bed, eyes rolling wildly as he muttered deranged gibberish under his breath. My gut clenched seeing his deteriorated condition.

"Mr. Sawyer?" I spoke gently, attempting to rouse him from his fugue state. "It's Dr. Blake. Can you hear me?"

In an instant, Sawyer's head whipped around, piercing me with a thousand-yard stare of sheer, bloodcurdling terror. His entire body went rigid as he unleashed a bone-chilling shriek that made my blood freeze in my veins.

"THEY'RE COMING!" he howled in primal fear, eyes bulging. "The shrouded ones - clawing their way through the veil of sleep to take us all!"

I recoiled in shock as his ravings dissolved into graphic, disturbing descriptions that made my mind reel. Sawyer appeared completely unhinged, lost in his horrific vision as he recounted in lurid detail:

"Twisted, gnashing monstrosities oozing through the cracks of reality! Their leering, soulless pits bore into my psyche, flaying all sense of reason and hope. Hooked talons and serrated fangs rendered flesh as they feasted upon our deepest, darkest dreads made manifest!"

His words painted such harrowing, unnatural pictures that my stomach churned with nauseous vertigo. Sawyer's face contorted into a mask of pure, unadulterated mania, spittle flying as he descended into further disjointed, animalistic shrieks.

"The dream harvesters come to reap our essence! Our dimensional tether frays as their looming presence bleeds through the fissures. All will be unmade!"

That's when he started thrashing about violently, seemingly in the throes of some unseen force accosting him. I shouted for assistance as orderlies rushed in to subdue and sedate the out-of-control patient. It took multiple burly men to finally wrestle Sawyer into restraints as he continued bucking and howling about the encroaching forces of nightmare.

I could only look on in stunned horror, his dire warnings of cosmic terror infiltrating our reality searing into my psyche. Had he truly glimpsed something unholy lurking beyond the veil of sleep? Or was this merely the raving of a shattered, fragile mind?

As they administered sedatives to finally calm his frantic struggle, I couldn't help but wonder if we were all going irreversibly mad here at Grimmwood. What fresh hell lurked behind those tormented eyes?

I stumbled back to my quarters in a daze after the harrowing ordeal with Sawyer, his haunting descriptions of dimensional nightmare beasts replaying on a sickening loop. My hands trembled as I shakily poured myself a glass of water, struggling to regain my composure.

What I had witnessed felt so viscerally real, and yet part of me recoiled at how utterly insane it all sounded. Monsters bleeding through the dream realm to harvest our psychic essence? It seemed like the stuff of deranged delusion and supernatural horror fiction, not grounded in any rational reality.

And yet…the way Sawyer had raved, contorted in abject terror - it chilled me to my core with how palpable his fear was. Those visions tormented him as surely as any waking threat. Who was I to dismiss it all as mere madness?

Desperate to reassure my buckling grip on reality, I turned to the stacks of files and research littering my desk. Laying it all out in an organized, analytical manner always helped center my clinical mindset.

But as I pored over the materials, the shadow of Sawyer's disturbing narratives crept into the periphery like ominous whispers in the dark. I found myself growing agitated and unable to concentrate, vivid flashes of gnashing maws and shrouded entities clouding my vision. My pen scratched increasingly erratic, trembling notations in the margins as fatigue and dread steadily sapped my faculties.

At some point, I must have drifted into a restless slumber, slouched over my desk. The next thing I knew, I was plunged into a vortex of surreal, nightmarish unreality that made my heart stampede with primal panic.

Disjointed images and half-formed monstrosities assaulted my senses from all sides in a kaleidoscope of terror. Sawyer's ravings coalesced into fleshy, unspeakable forms of weeping pus that seared my soul. All logic ladders disappeared as the dream realm subsumed any notion of rational grounding. I was untethered in a hellscape of twisting delirium and existential dread.

I awoke screaming, my cheek stuck to a pooled drool on the desk as I flailed in a cold sweat, unanchored between the disparate realms of fantasy and reality. What was a dream, and what was waking horror? Sawyer's warnings echoed in my mind, jumbling with half-glimpsed apparitions.

I must have sat there for an indeterminate span, simply staring vacantly and fighting the creeping sensation of psyche splintering. A torrent of deeply repressed, primordial fears roiled just beneath the surface now, threatening to unhinge my sanity completely.

In that fraught state of utter disassociation and existential vertigo, I honestly could not tell what was true anymore. Was I going as irrevocably mad as Sawyer, paranoid visions of cosmic evil infecting my subconscious? Or had I somehow cracked the surface of something ancient and terrible, permeating the boundaries we deluded ourselves existed between nightmare and reality?

In that tremulous moment, balanced on the precipice of losing myself completely, the only certainty was the yawning, encroaching spiral into deepening doubt of my own credibility and mental faculties. An uncomfortable uncertainty took root - was the threat external and metaphysical, or rooted in the internal psyche's descent into delusion?

The next morning, I was summoned to Dr. Blake's office with a stern look. His jaw was set in a hard line as he regarded me coldly from across his desk.

"Dr. Matthews, I've received multiple complaints about your unprofessional conduct last night," he stated in a clipped tone. "Your hysterics with Mr Sawyer were not only disruptive but seemed to agitate and frighten the other patients as well."

I opened my mouth to explain, to recount the sheer horror I had witnessed but Blake raised his hand to silence me.

"Your alarming outburst and screaming about monsters was entirely uncalled for. It simply fed into that poor man's psychosis and delusions."

Delusions? The way he so callously dismissed Sawyer's haunting visions made me second-guess everything I had seen and made me question my own grasp on reality.

"H-Have you been getting enough rest?" Blake's voice took on a patronizing tone as if speaking to a child. "This job can be quite stressful. Perhaps you're not getting sufficient sleep?"

"I...I've been having strange dreams," I started, feeling small under his domineering glare. "Horrible nightmares, tied to what Sawyer described about forces invading from some nightmare realm..."

Blake sighed heavily, pinching the bridge of his nose in obvious exasperation. "You're letting this silly nightmare nonsense get into your head. They're just bad dreams, nothing more."

His arrogant dismissal of my concerns about what could be something so much bigger, so much more cosmic and evil, stung deep. This was the man I had opened myself up to so vulnerably before, and now he patted me on the head like a confused child.

"Clearly, you're not handling the stress of this job well," Blake continued coldly. "You're having delusional paranoia from lack of sleep, making a professional matter overly personal and emotional."

My heart sank as he suggested, in so many words, that I was losing my grip on sanity and rationality. That my credibility was slipping along with my faculties over some foolish paranoia and obsession with patients' dreams.

"Perhaps it's best you take a leave of absence," he stated firmly, folding his hands on the desk. "Go home, get some rest, and regain your perspective before you have another unprofessional episode."

I could only stare back, feeling as if the man I had started to care for deeply had just slapped me across the face. His harsh rebuke and his invalidating gaslighting of my experiences and intuitions crushed me. If even he, my closest confidant here, thought me hysterical and delusional…what hope did I have of being taken seriously? Of stopping whatever sinister force I suspected?

I left Blake's office utterly deflated, my confidence in shreds. His harsh dismissal of my experiences and concerns made me question everything - my judgment, my perceptions, even my basic sanity. Was I truly just an overstressed workaholic becoming unhinged and paranoid? Doubts swirled in my mind like a murky whirlpool threatening to drown me.

I found myself wandering the halls in a daze, with no particular destination in mind. My steps were leaden, my spirit weighted by profound dejection. If I couldn't even get the man I cared for to take me seriously and consider there were deeper, metaphysical forces at play here, what chance did I have?

Somehow, I ended up outside the medical observation room where they were keeping Sawyer sedated and restrained. Despite his raving state earlier, the sight of him now gave me pause. There was something in his expression, a flicker of lucidity struggling against the forced fog of drugs.

Our eyes met through the reinforced window as he lolled his head toward me. In that fleeting moment, I witnessed a desperate urgency, a profound need to communicate and connect simmering behind his haunted gaze.

Sawyer mouthed something, garbled and indistinct through the barrier separating us. But there could be no mistaking the intention behind it - a warning, a revelation he needed me to heed before all was lost.

In a dizzying rush, the memory of his dire confessions about cosmic malignant forces breaching the veil of dreams into our realm came flooding back to me in visceral clarity. At the time, his litany of grotesque horrors had seemed the nonsensical ramblings of a fractured psyche.

But staring into his pleading, desperate eyes now, I experienced a chilling paradigm shift. What if Sawyer's mania was not mere delusion but rooted in a profound, terrifying truth? One my clinical mind rejected due to its seeming impossibility? The way he had accurately mirrored the escalating nightmares plaguing the other patients...

Suddenly, the veil dropped from my eyes as I realized Blake's gaslighting and condescension were not just arrogance - they were purposeful misdirection and deception cloaked in the veneer of clinical superiority. He wanted to contain what existed here, to brush it aside as delusion and coincidence. But deep down, he knew there were metaphysical realities and ancient evils lurking, ones he was complicit in somehow.

In that epiphany, my fear and self-doubt melted away, replaced by simmering anger and determination. I would not be deterred or dissuaded from the path Sawyer was beckoning me down, no matter how nightmarish the implications. If interdimensional entities truly did imperil our world, if the dream realm overlapped our own in ways we could scarcely comprehend, then it was my solemn duty to confront this head-on.

No longer would I entertain doubts about my sanity or credibility. John Sawyer's suffering, the cosmic terror reflected in his eyes—that was the purest truth I had witnessed. And I vowed to shine light into those shadowed spaces and defend reality itself, no matter the personal cost.

Turning on my heel, I marched with reinvigorated purpose toward the records room. It was time to truly delve into the blackest depths of Grimmwood's sordid history and lay bare any threads that unraveled into the nightmare abyss – before the walls between worlds dissolved forever.

CHAPTER 6

6

Clues from the Past

After my chilling interaction with the sedated Sawyer, a fire was lit within me. I could no longer dismiss or ignore the gnawing sense that there were deeper, darker forces at play here than simple delusion or madness. Blake's overt deception had confirmed my worst suspicions - something profoundly evil festered at the core of Grimmwood Manor.

I attacked the archival records and materials with an unslakable thirst for answers. File after file, account after account, I devoured with an increasingly frantic pace. My desperation grew with each passing hour as nightmarish puzzle pieces began taking shape in my mind's eye.

It was deep within the dusty annals of Grimmwood's primordial origins that I started to unravel the threads of the ancient, chthonic evil inlaid here. Short, seemingly innocuous asides mentioned the manor's construction atop far more archaic foundations - scattered archaeological references to ruins, carvings, and structures predating modern history.

At first, they appeared as mere curiosities and local folklore. But my attention was utterly ensnared when I came across the first etchings and illustrations from those excavated sites. My breath caught in my throat, an icy chill lancing my core.

The artwork, if one could call it that, depicted grotesque, indescribable iconography and symbols seemingly born of a reality completely alien to our own. Strange geometries and non-Euclidean formations blurred the line between the organic and inorganic in ways that instinctively repulsed and unsettled me.

These renderings of things did not belong to the known order of life as we understand it. There was an unmistakable sense of the profoundly unholy and anti-natural at work. They called to the primal, childlike part of my psyche that could only perceive them as "wrong" and psychically profane at a visceral level.

The longer I studied those blasphemous hieroglyphs and pictograms, the more palpable the ominous dread became. It was not mere superstitious paranoia inducing this creeping sense of cosmic menace—it was a deeper instinctual awareness that these sigils served as inscrutable ciphers to realities and dimensions that were too immense and horrible for humankind's limited perception to fully comprehend.

My sense of being a trespasser into forbidden, proscribed domains only escalated as I realized entire swaths of text and imagery were clearly redacted, blacked out with censorious intent. Someone had gone to calculated lengths to obscure elements of this archaic knowledge and iconography.

Who were they protecting—and from what precisely? The more I absorbed, the clearer it became that these finds predated and influenced everything Grimmwood had been constructed for: an age-old conspiracy to probe...or perhaps commune with...these immanent, malign forces.

As the scope of how deep and vast this hidden, subterranean history truly went, a sense of grim purpose solidified. I knew that to unearth the truth, to tear away the veil of willful ignorance and lies perpetuated here - I would have to delve quite literally into the shadows and foundations of what Grimmwood was erected upon.

No obstacle would deter me now. I was utterly committed to plunging down the metaphoric rabbit hole, wandering ever deeper into the waking nightmare no matter how psychically treacherous it became. Only by shining light into the most crepuscular reaches would I find the primal evil lurking there.

Even if that journey risked perilous impacts on my own tenuous grasp on reality itself, the cost of wilful blindness felt far steeper. For I recognized that whatever cosmic monstrosities threatened the boundaries of our waking world and unconscious realms had already sunk their talons into Grimmwood Manor.

With a pounding heart and trembling hands, I disabled the security systems and found my way into the long-sealed tunnels beneath Grimmwood. Ducking through narrow corridors thick with dust and cobwebs, every scrap of my footsteps reverberated loudly in the oppressive silence.

The dank, musty air felt heavier the deeper I descended, pressing in on me with the weight of untold antiquity. Banishing thoughts of getting trapped forever in these lightless, subterranean passages, I pressed onward with my meager flashlight, cutting a feeble come through the mothering blackness.

After what felt like an interminable journey inward, I emerged into a colossal, vaulted grotto of indeterminate size. The beam of my light could barely illuminate the perimeter, swallowed by encroaching gloom.

But what it did reveal, piecemeal, caused my breath to hitch - layer upon layer of intricate, disturbing carvings adorning every hewn surface. Stretching as far as my light could penetrate were sickening friezes and reliefs depicting... things...utterly antithetical to human comprehension or natural order.

At first, they appeared merely bizarre, esoteric symbols and iconography like I'd encountered in the ancient records. But the deeper I ventured, the more disturbing it became as the nature of the engravings coalesced into focus.

I was surrounded by visceral depictions of entities, beings, or presences so transgressive and antithetical to our reality that I shuddered involuntarily. Whatever created these carvings did so in an attempt to represent things not meant for human biologies to perceive. The geometries and dimensions endlessly fractured into incomprehensible new pathways antithetical to our perceptions of matter and existence itself.

Even more chilling, I found clear ritualistic imagery of humanoid sacrifices or subjugations intermixed with these star-spawned depictions. It became sickeningly apparent this was the work of an ancient, structured cult or practice involving invocations or beckoning to these immanent, cosmic monstrosities.

The scale of the carvings and chambers intimated a devotion and infrastructure far beyond my prior comprehension. This was not some fringe eccentricity but rather an organized veneration of and ritualistic probing towards forces malignantly apathetic to humanity's definition of reality.

As the sickening enormity of it all became apparent, a yawning sense of dread and revulsion hollowed me from within. My scholar's zeal curdled into horror at the implications that—for centuries, perhaps millennia—there existed focused attempts to erode the veil separating our world from that of the cosmic, delirium-born entities humanity was never meant to trade with.

My worst fears were confirmed when I happened upon archaic tomes and manuscripts strewn about, detailing accounts of interdimensional contacts, gateways, and attempted subjugation rituals with these entities. So many redacted portions of text and references became clear - this unholy site dated back centuries to an organized cult attempting to summon malefic entities from the nightmare dreamscape into our material reality.

In that sickening moment of revelation, my grip on sanity grew tenuous as I struggled against the psychic miasma of forces and entities too immense and non-Euclidean for any human mind to comprehend. If these texts and engravings were even partially accurate accounts, then I had indeed breached entryways into the abyss - one which now recognized and reacted to my witness.

As the cosmic horror of my surroundings coalesced, an unmistakable sense of psychic dread manifested - a palpable presence stirring in the primordial shadows. A miasma of psychic disturbance rippled through the stale airs as if my witness had triggered a lurking malignancy from its slumber.

The veil between realities, between dream and waking, grew gossamer thin in those dizzying moments. Unnatural phenomena flickered at the periphery - strange geometries refracting, spectral apparitions congealing from the occult etchings, pervasive whispers in a billion dead languages. My mind strained under the deluge of sensory overload from dimensions my feeble human perception could scarcely process.

I felt a palpable psychic bleed, an infiltration into my consciousness by dormant entities stirred from their stagnant vigil. Eons of somnolence ended as my third eye cracked open Pandora's abyss tied to the primordial planes of cosmic dreaming. Realms of meta-cosmic infinitum splintering off into endless parallel branchings of being and un-being.

At that moment, I experienced a synaptic meltdown as my perception was subsumed by the true, deeper reality underlying the pathetic, mundane existence we delude ourselves with daily. Visions of the dreaming multiverse assailed me - an eternal, churning marinade of infinite higher dimensions and incomprehensible geometries.

Our paltry four-dimensional reality proved merely the feeble periphery, the narrowest of waking minds dipping a single toe into the true cosmic maelstrom of perpetual dreaming. Layer upon layer of finitude nestled within one another across hyper-compressed fractal assistance, rendered in the lurid hues of worlds both beautifully embryonic and abjectly horrifying.

The scope of it all threatened to reduce my mind to burnt cinders. For our pitiful anthropocentric understanding was but a nanosecond's reverie, a mere blink in the slumbering consciousness of true BEING. One spun from the delirious fever dreams of incomprehensibly vast intelligence continually laboring to give birth to themselves across eternities.

Part of me shriveled away under the psychic onslaught, unmade by visceral awarenesses and cosmic revelations too immense for my fragile human ego to withstand. But another part, the deepest, most primal core of my essence, bore witness to something else stirring amidst the dreaming aethereal infinitudes.

A singularity, a point of infinite density where all light and rays of consciousness got bent, returning no coherent signal. An event horizon around sheer, primordial evil. Something ancient, feaster of souls, plague-born from the luminous depths of meta-reality's original dream screamed in ecstatic agony at being perceived once more by a waking mind.

In that searing nanosecond, I glimpsed the yawning, eternal maw of the Nightmare Lord, borrowed from the cosmic womb eons past. A resonance shuddered through reality in response to my witness, an unholy communion that flooded my cerebral cortex with the psychological equivalent of a ruptured aneurysm.

Only by exerting every fiber of psychic strain, disassociating my fraying grip on consciousness, did I narrowly avoid being subsumed into a waking nightmare from which there could be no escape. In that severing of perceptions, I blacked out just as this primordial monstrosity turned its full phenomenological awareness in my direction.

When I came to, huddled in a corner of the damned chamber in a cold sweat, the gravity of what primordial evil I'd stumbled into dawned with apocalyptic severity. My prior suspicions of interdimensional threats were but a candle's flicker compared to the eldritch sun blazing behind the veil of reality's dream.

I'd unearthed forbidden thresholds never meant to be crossed by the meager bandwidth of humanity's perceptual limitations. The naive shall tread the path of nightmares and know the true face of cosmic dread from which our dreamless slumbers provide scant protection.

7

Nightmares Become Real

Over the following days, something profoundly disturbing began happening with the patients at Grimmwood Manor. What started as seemingly isolated incidents soon revealed an unsettling pattern that chilled me to the bone.

Jenny, a young woman plagued by intense nightmares of grotesque, multi-limbed creatures attacking her, awoke one morning with a series of deep, oozing lacerations across her face. The gouges matched precisely the locations and lengths of the claw marks she described from her night terrors.

At first, the medical staff tried to explain it as self-inflicted wounds, perhaps from an undocumented night panic attack. But then Samuel, an elderly patient whose dreams involved falling into endless pits lined with rusted spikes, was found covered in strange, circular puncture wounds on his back and limbs. The injuries were exactly like the vicious impalements he recounted each morning after awakening.

One by one, more patients began appearing with external injuries that mirrored, in shocking detail, the horrific traumas they claimed to experience in their dream worlds night after night. Mangled flesh, deep slashes, bludgeoned bruises - all inexplicably manifesting on their physical bodies despite no plausible medical explanations.

A sense of frenzied panic quickly took hold as grotesquely new examples emerged with every sunrise. How was it possible for these people to sustain very real, visceral lacerations and bodily trauma from mere subconscious experiences within their minds while sleeping? The implications were profoundly unsettling.

I watched in growing horror and confusion as the gruesome wounds became more and more severe. Formerly minor scratches gave way to disfiguring gashes, then shocking displays of flayed flesh and protruding bone. It was as if the nightmare dimensions were seeping malignant tendrils into our reality, able to reach through to the dreaming patients and inflict tangible harm upon them.

The deranged ramblings I had so diligently analyzed and the profane etchings in that wretched underground chamber all corroborated the same disturbing notion - that these were not just feverish hallucinations. They were windows into an ether reality coexisting alongside our own, populated by predators and entities able to transcend realms.

By the time Samir was wheeled into the medical ward - his body a ravaged, unrecognizable tangle of flayed viscera so horrific it caused the entire intake staff to immediately break down into hysterics - I knew something was cosmically, terribly wrong. Whatever barriers had once separated our reality from the realm of perpetual nightmares were rapidly disintegrating.

The delirious, torturous dream states our patients suffered were no longer quarantined to the safety of the unconscious mind. The nightmare realm had begun bleeding into our waking existence, and we had no defenses against a dimension constructed from the very warped geometries of our primal dreads and fears made viscerally, traumatically manifest.

Adding to the disturbing phenomena of physical wounds from the ether, patients began reporting constant instances of being "summoned" from their sleep by otherworldly voices and presences. They would wake in the night, frantic and terrified, babbling about strange refrains beckoning them to some unknown, unseen place.

Old man Garcia was particularly haunted, swearing up and down that his deceased son had spoken to him through the dreamscape, plaintively calling for him to join him out in the woods surrounding the manor's grounds. The hollow desperation etched on Garcia's face as he recounted the young boy's pleas still chills me.

At first, the overnight staff simply dismissed such episodes as confused ramblings and senility. But then I, too, began hearing eerie, indistinct murmurs carried on the evening winds as I roamed the darkened pathways encircling the property.

An unnerving sense took hold that the boundaries separating our waking world from the encroaching nightmare realm frayed and thinned with each sun setting. Normal, linear dreaming devolved into a viscous haze - warp-spanned chronologies seeping across thresholds never meant to be breached.

Increasingly, it became impossible to tell if the wispy voices and shadow forms flickering at the corners of our eyes were external phenomena or insidious phantasms hijacking the winding backroads of our psyches from their dimension of perpetual dreaming.

With each night that passed, the tooth-and-nail struggle to retain a conviction in objective reality intensified. Unseeing forces untethered to our cloistered anthropocentric perspectives tugged at the very fabric of perceived existence, fraying it.

Dream and waking life blurred and bled across a continuum, leaving us unsure whether we moved gilded or trapped in yet another layer of IllusionSpun labyrinth. The semblance of anything solid and comprehensible slipped steadily through our grasping fingers like fistfuls of smoke.

A few nights later, in the early hours before dawn, the overnight staff was thrown into complete chaos and panic. One of our residents, Jacob Trumble, had simply vanished without a trace.

His room showed clear signs of a violent struggle - twisted sheets strewn about, a lamp lying shattered on the floor, and strange deep gouges scratched into the walls. The window was ajar, opening onto the dark, wooded grounds surrounding the manor.

Despite an immediate lockdown and exhaustive search of the entire premises, Jacob was nowhere to be found inside. A sickening dread gripped me as I assembled a small team to venture outside and follow the disturbing trail leading from his room into the blackness of the tree line.

Pushing through the thick underbrush and overhanging branches, we struggled to pick up Jacob's trail in the gloom. Our meager flashlight beams only served to make the shadows between the looming trunks seem to shift and writhe with unseen movement.

We had barely made it fifty yards when Jacob's blood-curdling screams suddenly pierced the night air. The agonized shrieks reverberated all around us, seeming to come from multiple impossible directions at once. The primal, existential terror in his pleas for help caused every hair on my body to stand on end.

As abruptly as the screaming began, it simply…stopped. The silence that followed was even more chilling as if a smothering blanket had been thrown over the entire forest. We frantically called out Jacob's name, our voices getting swallowed up by the obscuring darkness and density of the woodland.

No response came save for the mocking hoots of distant owls and…an encroaching murmur. A steady, indistinct susurration that seemed to issue from all around us, just below the cusp of coherent perception. A deeply unsettling sense took hold that innumerable, unseen eyes keenly observed us.

Despite every instinct screaming at us to turn back, we pressed onwards. The only path left to follow now were the cryptic gouges and claw marks leading off the trail as if something had dragged Jacob further into the stygian heart of the forest.

After what felt like an eternity lost in that lightless, arboreal labyrinth, we finally found Jacob. But the sight that unfolded before us is seared into my memory forever - a vision of cosmic, existential dread that still wakes me in cold sweats.

Our feeble flashlight beams revealed Jacob hovering ten feet above the loamy forest floor, his body suspended and rigid as if gripped by some unseen force. He was being inexplicably drawn upwards, pulled in a slow, inexorable trajectory towards a shimmering oval anomaly that seemed to warp and undulate in the air before us.

At first, I thought it was some strange lighting artifact, a swirling miasma of fog playing tricks on our eyes. But as we inched cautiously closer, it became horrifyingly apparent that this was no mere optical illusion - it was a tear in the very fabric of reality itself.

Through the puckered, oval-shaped rift, we caught disturbing glimpses of scenery identical to our very surroundings - only...wrong. Familiar trees and foliage warped into approximations that shouldn't be possible, their geometries refracted through some other spatial dimension. Gravity itself appeared to puddle and eddy in unsettling defiance of the natural laws we understood.

But most harrowing of all were the appendages gripping Jacob, reeling him with steady torque towards the void's starving aperture. Smoky, midnight-black tendrils that flicked and wriggled with unsettling, alien sentience, sporting profane geometries, and logic-defying angles more akin to those wretched friezes in the occult ruins beneath the manor.

They wrapped Jacob in their grip with a disturbing simultaneity of sadistic frenzy and cold indifference. His upturned face contorted in an anguished rictus of primal, existential horror, golden streams of panic spittle frozen in the air around him.

In those final moments before the inevitable, Jacob's eyes locked with mine. A nanosecond of shared, unutterable dread and communion. He knew. We both knew what was inescapably coming.

Then, with a violent SLURP, as if all atmosphere were vacuumed inside itself, the outer periphery of Jacob's torso breached the mercurial, puckered lip of the rift. For a fraction of a second, I could see...something...on the other side. A presence so cosmically antithetical to all natural order, my feeble biological hardware could only strain to interpret its mere existence before shutting down completely.

With one final soul-sundering choker-gag, Jacob vanished fully through the gaping maw. The aperture then contracted with a sick, wet burp, reknitting the boundaries of our reality as seamlessly as a wound cauterized - except leaving behind nothing but a haunting pile of scattered crimson flecks, slowly seeping into the soil.

Just like that, the nightmare realm had physically manifested to claim one of our own. The madness was no longer confined to dreams - its bony fingers now gripped the waking world as well, unhinging reality from all our foolish anthropocentric assumptions of rationality and order.

In that moment of shared cosmic dread, I had been force-fed a brimming dosage of the sheer existential insignificance plaguing our reality. That we are not masters of our domain at all...but mere morsels suspended in a primordial ooze of perpetual dreaming from which we can never awaken.

From the moment Jacob was unceremoniously slurped through that unholy rift, my tenuous grip on coherent dreaming rapidly unraveled. Nightmares ceased having discernible beginnings or endings, instead bleeding endlessly into one another like a Mobius strip of unremitting psychological torment.

One moment, I would jolt awake, drenched in chilled panic sweat, from a vision of being inescapably paralyzed in my quarters - an unseen, malevolent force steadily constricting my chest cavity with the inexorable, compressive strength of a caving star's gravity force. Just as the vise threatened to pulp my organs into an amorphous paste, the scene would suddenly dissolve and refract into an Escheresque hellscape.

The corridors outside my room extended into fleshy, labyrinthine grotesqueries looping back on themselves in ways that set my hindbrain ablaze with primal, nameless dread. My childhood home's familiar geometries blasphemously kaleidoscoped into non-Euclidean angles and tesseract convolutions never meant for biological minds to perceive.

At all hours of day or night, the barriers between dreaming and waking ceased having any coherent delineation. With no respect for linear chronology visions, and scenarios would simply...intrude...bleeding across unconscious thresholds like airborne spores of delirium. My already fraying grasp on any semblance of objective reality grew more unstable by the minute.

Increasingly, I found myself having strange moments of lucidity spanning both realms - a waking dream state of existential unreality where inner and outer sensory inputs merged into an undifferentiated soup. I'd be having a casual conversation when suddenly the person's voice began echoing in a pulsing reverberation, their features melting into abstract smears of color and form.

Or, while brushing my teeth, the mirror would gradually accrete a viscous, ink-black patina across its reflective surface. When I stared into the lightless void, I could have sworn a pair of fathomless, inhuman eyes slowly materialized to meet my horrified gaze.

I lived in perpetual uncertainty over whether I moved gilded through waking events or remained entrapped in yet another Escher-spun Möbius of illusion, dreaming all of existence into fleeting, bioluminescent coherence. Genuine reality and solipsistic hallucination grew impossible to tease apart, the connective threads spooling separately into my awareness completely frayed.

It was only a matter of dwindling time before the nightmare realm itself achieved its beachhead, piercing the veil to seed its terrifying ambassadors upon the corporeal plane. And the initial emissary was more psyche-shatteringly dire than I could ever have braced for.

One fateful evening, while I was doing routine paperwork, the air around me incrementally curdled and lost coherence. At first, I thought my vision was simply wavering due to eye strain or a migraine aura. But as the shimmering instability steadily worsened, a distinct sense of ominous, deliberate intent took palpable form.

The atmosphere itself seemed to be discoloring into a gossamer patina of oily, multi-hued iridescence. Before my disbelieving eyes, the amorphous miasma steadily thickened and congealed into a solid, roiling cloud of inky, vaporous maleficence.

The miasma sloughed insidiously towards me, belching occasional tendrils of like-fracted particulate that induced acrid, psychogenic effluvia. The noxious emissions wormed directly into my cerebral cortex, igniting synaptic wildfire in regions dating back to our primordial, single-celled ancestry on the ocean floors.

My entire being shuddered with innate revulsions at the sheer wrongness taking material shape before me. Every atavistic instinct screamed that I was in the presence of something far older, far more cosmically antithetical to the mere three-pound biological hardware I called consciousness.

As I watched in a stupor of abject, primal terror, the amorphous darkness began to slowly accrete into a roughly humanoid silhouette, upright and vaguely bipedal. Two cavernous, eyeless runnels appeared like gashes of abject vacuum carved directly into the Anguilla shroud, regarding me with the cold indifference of a celestial singularity.

My frantic heartbeat thundered in my ears as a gurgling, alien exhaling reverberated with eldritch physiologies. The shadowy avatar drew closer on appendages seemingly re-written from our spatial dimensions with each lurching step.

I wanted to scream, to run, to call for help - but my mind went rigid, utterly paralyzed with primal, synapse-deep dread. My fight-or-flight reflex simply blue-screened before the trespass of infinity, wearing our limited dimensionality like skin-sewn rags.

As the void spawn presence closed the remaining distance, I felt the interlocking tetrahedral layers of my psyche steadily disassociating one by one. My identity, my sense of discrete bodily selfhood, leached away into the oblivion of this ancient, dreaming maleficence.

Just when I thought the utter evacuation of my soul's essence into the cosmic waking nightmare was complete, the entity seemed to…INHALE. An abyss-born miasma thick with the residual dread of a billion eons of tormented sentience rushed directly into my feebly sparking synapses.

I jolted violently back to consensus reality with a primal, haunting scream - but it no longer mattered which side of the dreaming veil shuddered around me. The boundaries were irreparably breached, the distinctions hopelessly smeared.

Waking reality and perpetual nightmare had become a singular, undifferentiated state of being. And peering in from the peripheries of my electrified consciousness, the Outer Monstrosities now feasted without impediment on their latest transdimensional harvest.

My existential cries joined the echoing, eternal chorus in their lightless, delirium-spun abattoir. I had become fully subsumed, another mindstream subducted into the nihilistic event horizon of the dream's yawning malice.

CHAPTER 8

64

8

Confronting the Darkness

For weeks, little things about Dr. Hayden didn't add up: his weird looks sometimes, his vague comments about "higher callings." But I ignored the signs, too smitten by his charm and good looks—until I found that book.

I was searching his office late one night for a file. There, stuffed behind a bookcase, sat a black, leather-bound tome. Its pages were filled with bizarre symbols and depraved illustrations. Rituals for contacting entities from… somewhere else. Another dimension, maybe? It made my skin crawl just flipping through it.

I should have taken it directly to the police, but I foolishly confronted Daniel first, and the pit in my stomach grew. He had some explaining to do.

"This book details occult practices, Daniel. What's it doing here? What have you been up to?" I demanded, slamming it on his desk.

At first, he played dumb. Then his mask slipped, and a cruel, fanatic light flickered in his eyes.

"Don't you see, Anna? This is our great chance, our destiny," he said, voice dripping with fervor. "The gateway between realms can be reopened. We can be the next to walk those pathways."

My head spun. Pathways? Reopened? What nonsense was he spouting?

Daniel moved closer, looming over me with zeal. "The predecessors at Grimmwood only caught glimpses through the rift. But I know the way to pry it open fully."

He traced a finger along my cheek, and I recoiled. "You were always meant to be the final offering, my dear, to serve as the bridge between worlds."

Icy tendrils of dread gripped me then. This whole time, every lingering glance and whispered endearment had been a ploy. I was just a pawn in his deranged schemes to resurrect occult forces.

"Dr. Evans, I need you to come quick," Daniel said, voice tense over the intercom. "It's Steven Peters - he's having another major episode. I could use your help restraining him."

Lies. All lies. But I didn't know that yet as I hurried down the dim basement corridors towards the east wing's isolation rooms.

"Daniel?" I called out, finding the hall deserted. A faint rumbling seemed to emanate from up ahead.

Rounding the corner, I felt a sinking panic. A heavy steel door I'd never noticed before was swinging open, flickering torchlight glimmering from within. Against every instinct, I pressed forward.

The cloying stench of smoke and incense choked me as I descended a spiral staircase into…into what? Some kind of vast subterranean chamber carved directly from the bedrock. Disturbing sigils and incomprehensible glyphs adorned the walls, looking less like decorations and more like…summonings.

There! In the center, a looming ritualistic dais, lit by guttering braziers and ringed by black-robed, chanting figures. Leading them in a frenzied cadence was Daniel himself, arms raised high like a demented pastor.

"The signs converge at last! The pathways shall be reopened, the nightmare realm awakened!" he howled, spittle flying from his contorted face.

I opened my mouth to scream, to demand he stop this madness. But rough hands seized me from behind, more hooded acolytes rushing forth to restrain my thrashing.

They half-carried, half-dragged me towards the obsidian altar at the chamber's heart. Its slab was graven with a twisted glyph, one I realized too late mirrored the markings staining the cover of the disturbing tome.

I kicked and fought with every fiber of strength as they wrenched my limbs onto that blasphemous stone surface. Coarse ropes bound me at the wrists, ankles, and even my thrashing torso until I was utterly immobilized, a sacrificial offering to be made.

Daniel stalked the circumference, giddy as the chanting peaked around us in an eldritch crescendo. He seized an ornate, curved dagger and brandished it with wild ceremony.

I was lost, drowning in a waking nightmare made terribly, viscerally real. Beyond escape or rescue now. As the blade began its descent towards my bared chest, I could only squeeze my eyes shut, whimpering futile pleas.

The wicked dagger hung in the air, poised to pierce my heart and spill my blood. Daniel's face twisted with rapturous glee, the culmination of his madness playing out before my helpless eyes.

Then…a thunderous fracturing sound like reality itself was splitting asunder! The ground buckled and convulsed, sending the robed fanatics stumbling. A brilliant, ethereal rift ripped open behind the altar, pulsating tendrils of iridescent energy clawing outwards.

An unearthly howling pierced my eardrums, the eldritch gale whipping forth from the rupture carrying profane whispers and ghostly wails. Daniel turned towards the growing maelstrom, mouth agape in awe and terror. This was clearly beyond even his demented desires.

Black, smoky forms began coalescing amidst the maelstrom - humanoid shapes but…wrong, distorted in ways that grated my sanity. Their presence seemed to suck all light and hope from the chamber as they slithered forth.

The panicked cultists fled in blind terror, robes cast aside as they stampeded for the exits. In the confusion, the ropes binding me went slack, and I wrenched free with a primal surge of adrenaline.

I tumbled from the dais, greeted by a whirlwind of fractured, soul-scouring visions – cities of cyclopean obsidian, cosmic vortexes of gibbering matter, and vast formless presences hovering at reality's threshold.

Daniel was howling, incoherent ravings urging the insensate things to take me, to claim their "rightful vessel." Claws of vacuous force groped outwards, drawing me inexorably toward the pulsating rift.

With a breathless scream, I hurled myself into the eldritch maelstrom. There was no other choice - remain and be devoured by the void-spawned horrors or…or what? Oblivion seemed the better prospect compared to their endless, mind-rending embrace.

I was sucked through a kaleidoscope of light and fractal unrealities shattering all perception. Blinding chromaticism and alien geometry assailed my senses until blackness mercifully claimed me. When I awoke, it was to a desolate new realm of decay and paradox terror.

Swirling visions assaulted me, nightmarish landscapes flickering past in a delirium of madness. Charred cities warped into diseased spiral towers that oozed putrid ichor. Skies split open to reveal gaping maws of teeth and endlessly gibbering tongues.

I tumbled helplessly through this kaleidoscope of torment until finally expelled onto a scorched, lifeless plain. Hunks of shattered obsidian jutted up like broken glass over the endless ashen expanse. Twisted spires in the distance clawed at a dead, monochrome sky.

Staggering to my feet, the air felt heavier somehow—sicker. It felt like invisible terrors hung suspended all around in loathsome geometry. An ethereal droning reverberated through me, the unnatural hum of malign sentience scraping against my sanity.

In the far distance, anguished shrieks pierced the gloom - desperate calls of beings trapped in eternal torment echoing across this nightmare made it terribly real. They cried out futile warnings for me to flee, to escape while I still could.

But flee where? I spun in maddened circles, every inhuman structure and horizon holding equal menace. Whatever insanity spewed me forth into this desolation clearly hadn't intended for me to survive long after.

I had to move through. Had to try outrunning the steadily mounting sense of dread saturating every fiber of my being. That paralyzing certainty that while I may be alone for now, I wouldn't remain so for long.

Fixing on a slanted path between the obsidian shards, I broke into a stumbling lope, lungs scorched by the tainted atmospheres. Every few steps, I risked glancing over my shoulder, fraught with a premonition that some profane horror would soon be slithering in pursuit.

What unknown hells had I thrown myself into? What Stygian abominations now hungered for the warm meat of an unwitting trespasser? My mind straining against terrifying possibilities, I ran blindly towards any distant oblivion that might mercifully end my torment.

9

Realm of Nightmares

I fall through the rip between worlds, landing hard in a twisted, scary place that hurts my eyes and nose. The air is thick and smells really bad, like something rotten and dead. Tall, sharp black rocks spike up toward the red, angry sky that glows overheard. Below me, a bubbling sea of thick, tar-like goop sloshes around noisily. The stink makes me want to throw up, and it's hard to keep my mind here.

Everywhere I look, half-formed monster things lurk in the shadows - shapes with gnashing teeth, raking claws, and dripping icky slime. This whole place feels like a living example of all the fears and bad dreams people have swept under the rug. I know I must keep moving forward into this ever-changing world of horrors, even though every step makes me want to run away.

Twisted, melted creatures skitter just out of sight all around me. Large piles of bones and rotting flesh litter the ground, buzzing with flies. Things with too many eyes and mouths filled with needle teeth seem to be watching me from the inky black puddles. Gusts of putrid wind carry high-pitched laughter and muffled screams. My heart pounds in my ears as I try not to be sick from the smells.

I have to be brave and push deeper into this waking nightmare world. Even though it's the last place I want to be, people are trapped here suffering. If I don't find them a way out soon, who knows what terrors this place will unleash next. I take a deep breath of the foul air and start walking.

The twisty, nightmare land keeps changing shapes with every step I take like it's making fun of me. Sometimes I have to walk through deep puddles of burning acid goop that stings and hurts my legs. Other times, the ground turns into sharp pieces of black rock that cut into my feet and make me bleed.

All around me, I hear the terrible screaming sounds of people in horrible pain. The shrieking cries echo from every direction, bouncing inside my head until I feel like I'm going crazy. Up ahead, I see huge, lumped-together monsters that look like sickening, nightmarish versions of people's biggest fears.

There are massive swarms of bugs bigger than cars, clicking their pinchy mouth-legs together. There are armies of skeleton warrior creatures marching endlessly with swords and arrows. The worst ones are the melting disease-ridden blobs of guts and wounds that somehow slither around like they're alive. I want to be sick just looking at them.

I realize now that this whole place is like an evil nursery, where all the scary thoughts and fears people try to ignore get brought to life as a living, breathing bad dreams. No matter where I go, I can't escape the horrors springing up from the darkest corners of human minds.

Every once in a while, I find a tiny safe spot where the madness doesn't seem as bad for a moment. Dried-up old trees with bony branches give a little bit of cover to hide behind. Broken arches made of twisted animal bones let me catch my breath. But I always hear the slithering and scratching noises getting closer, reminding me the nightmare monsters are still out there hunting me.

I see creepy things carved into the rotten landscape, like curses and demonic signs warning me to stay away. The little safer spots never last long before more bad dreams come oozing out of the cracks. The demon creatures are always watching, waiting for me to let my guard down so they can pounce. I have to keep moving if I want to survive this maze of terrifying beings.

After what feels like forever being lost in this nightmare maze of terrible things, I finally reach a huge cavern. In the middle is a gigantic, ugly statue of me with my eyes sewn shut and mouth stuck wide open in a never-ending scream. I know right away this disturbing monument is a representation of my deepest fears and doubts about myself. To get out alive, I have to face and conquer the darkness inside my own mind.

Voices start whispering awful things at me from every direction, hissing mean put-downs and insults I've heard over and over again through the years. "You're just not good enough…you're broken…you're a failure…" They repeat all the cruel taunts from old classmates, the hurtful things exes said to me, and most painfully, the constant stream of toxic self-hatred from my own inner thoughts.

Shadowy figures with the faces of my loved ones appear, glaring at me with hate-filled eyes and spitting more painful criticisms that reopen old emotional wounds. Part of me wants to just collapse and give up under the huge weight of all this self-doubt and loathing I've carried for so long. But then I remember the missing patient who is counting on me to rescue them…all the innocent people who will suffer terribly if I can't find a way to seal this evil dimension off forever.

Feeling determined, I push back against each nasty voice by affirming positive truths about myself out loud. I confront the demons head-on with the facts I've fought so hard to accept - that I am stronger than their insults and that I am a worthy person despite my flaws. With every powerful statement of self-love, another cracked limb breaks off the massive ugly effigy.

One by one, I tear down and dismantle the twisted statue through sheer force of positive self-belief until it finally totters and shatters into pieces with an unearthly, bone-chilling screech. As the physical manifestation of all my doubts crumbles, I feel an unfamiliar sense of peace and lightness wash over me for the first time.

Just as I'm about to figure out where to go next in this cursed nightmare world, I hear a faint cry for help. It's the voice of the patient who went missing first! I run quickly towards the sound, dodging the snapping tentacles and whipping arms of nasty monsters stirred up by the noise.

I find the missing patient curled up and shaking in a small crack in the ground. Her eyes look empty, and her body is scary skinny - she's been trapped here for weeks, maybe even months. Her hospital gown is ripped and stained with gross, unspeakable filth. She flinches away when I approach, thinking I'm another demon coming to hurt her.

"It's okay, it's me, Dr. Peters from Grimmwood clinic," I say gently, helping her shakily stand up. "We must find a way out of this terrible place fast."

The poor patient can barely speak, her voice is so hoarse and raspy. She croaks a warning: "They're coming…the harbingers…"

Suddenly, a massive, earth-shaking boom rumbles throughout the nightmare realm. The bubbling tar pits start churning and splashing even crazier than before. Towering monster shapes start pulling themselves free of the thick goop - terrifying combinations of hands, hooks, teeth, and blades all mashed together in one terrible form.

These are the Harbingers, the vanguard of humanity's worst fears and nightmares given physical form. They've sensed the little spark of hope that me and the patient represent, and now they're coming for us. We have to run or be snuffed out for good.

I pull the stumbling, traumatized patient along as we flee from the charging tide of gnashing jaws and stabbing spikes erupting from the Harbingers. Between her ragged, panicked breaths, she shouts frantic warnings.

"They come from the Fear Caldera…a portal to even worse levels of terror and torment…we have to seal it off, or every human will get pulled into this endless nightmare!"

We scramble over the rotting, crumbling landscape as the Harbingers swarm after us, an unstoppable army of fangs and slithering dread. No matter how fast we run, I can feel their hot, rancid breath on our necks as more keep appearing.

10

Gateway Home

I could feel the bad feeling in the air getting stronger the closer we got to the gateway home. A darkness was growing all around us. Something evil and hateful.

My heart was beating fast. I knew we were going to have to fight the Nightmare Lord really soon. There was no way around it now. Part of me was very scared, but another part was determined to beat this evil thing once and for all. It had caused so much trouble and hurt so many people. It needed to be stopped.

The fear inside me felt like a little voice saying, "Run away! Go back! You'll never win against something so powerful and scary!" But I told that voice to be quiet. I couldn't run from this. If I didn't face the Nightmare Lord, the evil would just keep spreading, and more innocent people would get hurt.

I looked over at Sara, my brave friend who had been by my side through everything in this crazy nightmare world. The look on her face told me she was just as nervous as I was but just as committed to seeing this through. We didn't need to say anything - one look, and we both knew this was it. This was the big fight we had been preparing for. No matter how afraid we were, we would give it everything we had. The stakes were higher than any of us could imagine. But if we won, reality itself would finally be safe again.

I took a deep breath and gripped my sword tightly. Here we go.

When we finally got to the gateway site, it was super quiet and still. Too quiet. I could feel something bad was coming just from how eerie and dreadful the silence felt.

Then, all of a sudden, the ground started shaking like there was an earthquake! Me and Sara stumbled, trying hard not to fall over. From the middle of the gateway, we saw a huge shadowy shape start to appear and push its way through.

At first, it just looked like a big dark blob. But then it kept growing and changing shape until finally, the full monster emerged. My jaw dropped open when I saw what the Nightmare Lord really looked like. It was the most terrifying, twisted thing I had ever seen—like a million scary things all mashed up into one giant beast.

Sharp fangs, drooling jaws, horns, and claws extended in every direction from its pulsating body. Beady little eyes seemed to stare right into my soul. I wanted to run away screaming.

But then the Nightmare Lord reared back and let out the loudest, most bone-chilling roar. It felt like the sound could crack reality itself. Like a thousand nightmares, all screaming at once right into my brain.

I'm not ashamed to say I nearly pissed myself right then. Sara did, too, from the look on her face. We were both whimpering, paralyzed by ultimate terror for what felt like an eternity.

But then Sara's eyes met mine, and I could see her forcing her fear down and hardening her resolve. I did the same, taking a few deep breaths to calm myself. We had to be brave.

Without a word, we started quickly gathering our gear and weapons, trying to pull ourselves together enough to fight. As the Nightmare Lord advanced with thunderous steps, we exchanged a final glance and nodded. Here we go.

I lashed out with my sword for the first strike, a glancing blow across its grotesque form. It retaliated instantly with a sweep of razor claws. We had stepped over the threshold now. The ultimate battle had begun.

With that first exchange of blows, the real battle kicked into high gear. It was like nothing I had ever experienced before. Our attacks against the Nightmare Lord's terrible form shook the very ground and air around us. Reality itself seemed to be trembling and warping from the forces unleashed.

I slashed and hacked with my sword, aiming for any opening in that nightmarish mass of fangs, claws, and drooling mouths. But each time I struck, a barrage of spiky tendrils or sweeping claws came whipping back at me. I narrowly dodged repeatedly, the wind from those strikes ruffling my hair.

Through it all, Sara fought by my side as an incredible force. We had spent so much time battling together that we moved in perfect unison without even thinking about it. If I attacked high, she instantly went low. When I defended, she struck. Our moves created a continuous barrage that flowed like water.

But for all our ferocity and coordination, it still felt like we were hardly scratching the surface of this ancient evil. The Nightmare Lord's power seemed to stretch on forever into an abyss of darkness and despair. Just being near it made my senses reel, and my perception of reality got all twisted and funhouse-mirrored.

There were so many times when we came terribly close to having our last moments in this world. Rows of dripping fangs extended to engulf me. A solid wall of whipping tendrils appears from nowhere to smash Sara. We pulled through each time by the thinnest margins, battered and gasping for air.

With each fresh onslaught from this inexhaustible engine of malice, a new flicker of doubt took root within me. Could we actually prevail against such an ancient, primordial force of darkness? A lifetime of nightmares compacted into one all-consuming entity?

I looked over at Sara, her face straining and eyes wide with terror yet still brimming with determination to keep fighting. At that moment, I knew she was wondering the exact same thing. I gave her a nod to show I was still with her despite my doubts.

We had no choice but to pour every last drop of our strength and courage into this battle. If we faltered even a little against this eons-old entity of fear and horror, it would finally blast through our defenses and consume us and all of reality. There could be no surrender.

After what felt like an eternity of nonstop clashing and battling, we reached a moment when things seemed to pause. Sara and I were on one side, battered but still standing. The Nightmare Lord loomed over us, its countless limbs and mouths hung open, dripping black ooze. For a few seconds, nobody moved a muscle.

Sara took that brief moment to lock eyes with me. I could see the exhaustion on her face, but her eyes still burned with that unshakable spirit that had carried us so far.

"Don't you see?" she said between labored breaths. "This is what we're fighting for. Not just for ourselves, but for truth, light, goodness…for reality itself!"

Her words sliced through the fear and doubt, clouding my mind like a sword through fog. She was right. This was the ultimate battle between the forces of light and darkness, good and evil. As hopeless as it seemed, we had to keep fighting with everything we had.

I gave her a fierce nod of renewed determination. But just then, a fresh wave of horror washed over me as I saw the Nightmare Lord's putrid from beginning to shift and contort again.

Before I could react, a half-dozen slimy tendrils whipped out and coiled themselves around Sara's arms and legs with unbreakable strength. She cried out in shock as the bonds started dragging her inexorably across the ground towards the still-open gateway.

"No!!" I screamed an animalistic wail that scratched my throat raw. I charged forward, hacking wildly at the restraints, but they simply absorbed every blow, reconstituting behind my strikes instantly.

The Nightmare Lord turned what passed for its loathsome face towards me. Though it had no visible mouth, an echoing laugh reverberated from its core straight into my skull. With a gesture that made my brain feel like it was being wrung out, it renewed its efforts to pull Sara through the gateway.

Time seemed to slow to a crawl as our eyes met one final time. I saw Sara's face shift from shock and fear to an expression of sorrowful acceptance, but also a love for me that outshone any of the horror surrounding us at that moment—as if to say, "It's okay."

Then, like a silent supernova, a brilliant azure light exploded outwards from Sara's body. When it cleared, I could abruptly sense what needed to be done. I knew I couldn't allow that creature to drag Sara's light fully into the darkness between realities. Not after everything.

My course was set.

I couldn't let the fear and horror of that moment break me. Sara was counting on me. Reality itself was at stake. I took a deep breath and steadied my shaking hands around my sword's hilt.

With every last ounce of strength left in my body, I gathered my power and focused it into a single strike. When the moment was right, I let out a feral yell and swung my blade in a sweeping arc at the gateway itself behind the Nightmare Lord's grotesque form.

The blow struck true, shearing through the gateway's very structure. Cracks of blue energy began spreading rapidly across its surface as it started to fracture and splinter apart.

After a shocked pause, the Nightmare Lord seemed to realize what was happening. Its path of retreat, its way to fully cross over into our world, was being severed. A deafening screech of anger and confusion emanated from the beast as ghostly tendrils flailed wildly.

In that instant, before everything collapsed, I could lock eyes one last time with Sara's ensnared form. Even though no words could be exchanged, I could read the expression on her beautiful face as clearly as if they were etched in stone.

I am grateful for giving my all to stop this evil.
    Pride in how far we had come together against insurmountable odds.
    But most of all, an infinite, transcendent love that made my heart swell and

eyes sting.

Then the gateway ruptured in a blinding explosion, banishing the Nightmare Lord back through the rift with a shriek tinged with what I could have sworn was the first true fear I'd ever heard from it. Our worlds were finally sealed off for good as the gaps closed around the creature's crackling form.

I stood alone amid the eerie silence that followed. The evil had been vanquished from our reality…but at the cost of Sara's eternal entrapment in the nightmare realm, her light snuffed out.

A hollow, bittersweet victory. I had saved the world, but lost everything that truly mattered to me. As I awaited my eventual return home, I knew no one there could ever understand the unfathomable struggles I had endured.